ROBOTS™

RODNEY
GOES
TO TOWN

By Acton Figueroa

HarperKidsEntertainment
An Imprint of HarperCollins*Publishers*

In a little place called Rivet Town,
a little robot named Rodney Copperbottom
was made.

As Rodney grew, he needed bigger parts,
like every growing robot.
But parts cost a lot of money.
Rodney always got hand-me-down parts
from his cousins.
He did not mind.

Like lots of little bots,
Rodney loved *The Bigweld Show*.
Bigweld was Rodney's hero.
He watched the show every week.
Rodney wanted to be an inventor,
just like Bigweld.

Every year there was a big parade
in Rivet Town.
Every year Rodney and his dad
went to the parade.
Rodney loved to watch the balloons go by—
especially the Bigweld balloon.

"One day I am going to visit Bigweld!"
Rodney said.

At the end of his show, Bigweld says that the
gates of Bigweld Industries are always open.

"All I have to do is go to the gates
and Bigweld will listen to my ideas."
Rodney's dad smiled when he heard
his son's dream.

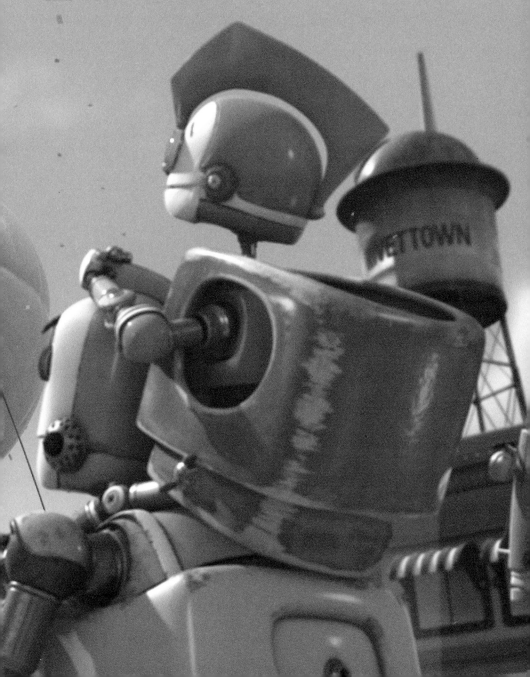

Rodney kept dreaming.

He also kept working on his big invention—
the Wonderbot.

But when he grew up,

Rodney had to get a job.

Rodney went to work with his dad.
Mr. Copperbottom was a dishwasher
at a restaurant.

Rodney was not happy at the restaurant.
He wanted to invent things and
work on the Wonderbot.

Rodney decided to combine what he
wanted to do with what he had to do.
He figured out a way to have
the Wonderbot help his dad.

Mr. Copperbottom was always busy
at the restaurant.

Sometimes he had to take work home.

Rodney figured that if the Wonderbot helped,
his dad would not have to work so hard.

But things did not work out the way
Rodney thought they would.
Everything started out okay.
Then, instead of helping his dad,
the Wonderbot made a mess of things.
Dishes shattered everywhere.

Mr. Copperbottom tried to explain to his boss,
Mr. Gunk, what had happened.
The Wonderbot did not mean
to break any dishes!
But no matter what Mr. Copperbottom said,
his boss would not stop yelling.

Mr. Gunk was angry.

He was so angry

that he fired Rodney on the spot.

"I want your son

out of my restaurant!" he yelled.

Rodney did not get upset.

He decided he was ready to leave Rivet Town
and go meet Bigweld.

He wanted to share his ideas.

Most of all, he wanted to show Bigweld
his big invention.

Rodney's mom did not want him to leave. "But everyone in town hates me!" Rodney said. "That is not true," Rodney's mom replied. Just then a newspaper bot walked by calling out the latest headline: "READ ALL ABOUT IT! EVERYBODY HATES HIM!"

Rodney's dad understood his desire
to become an inventor.

"This is his dream," Mr. Copperbottom
told his wife.

"We have to let him go."

Rodney's dad bought him a train ticket
to Robot City.
Rodney hugged his parents and climbed onboard.
As the train left the station, he waved good-bye.
He was on his way!

WELCOME TO ROBOT CITY, read

a giant sign.

It was the first thing Rodney saw.

Rodney was excited.

He knew that Bigweld could not be far away!

Everywhere Rodney looked,
robots rushed from here to there.
Robot City was *nothing* like Rivet Town.
Rodney saw livery bots—they took bots from
the train station to where they needed to go.
Next, Rodney saw a dancing bot.

Rodney even saw an information bot.

He asked it for directions.

The information bot was happy to help.

Rodney soon found the train

that would take him to his hero, Bigweld.

It was not like any train

Rodney had ever seen before!

Following the signs,

Rodney saw a huge escalator.

He walked onboard and up, up, up it went.

There was nothing like this

in Rivet Town, either.

Robot City was full of surprises!

Suddenly, Rodney was scooped up

and dropped into another vehicle.

His car slammed into another one just like it.

The cars shot straight down

like a roller coaster.

Down and up, in and out,

Rodney's car zoomed along like a rocket.

When the car slowed to a stop,

Rodney got out.

He was a bit shaky from the ride,

but still very excited.

Then he looked up.

Rodney stared at the gates he knew so well.

Rodney had made it all the way
to Bigweld Industries!
Now his dreams would come true—
Rodney would finally meet his hero, Bigweld!